Stephanie Stansbie • Polona Lovsin

WHAT'S THAT NOISE, LITTLE MOUSE?

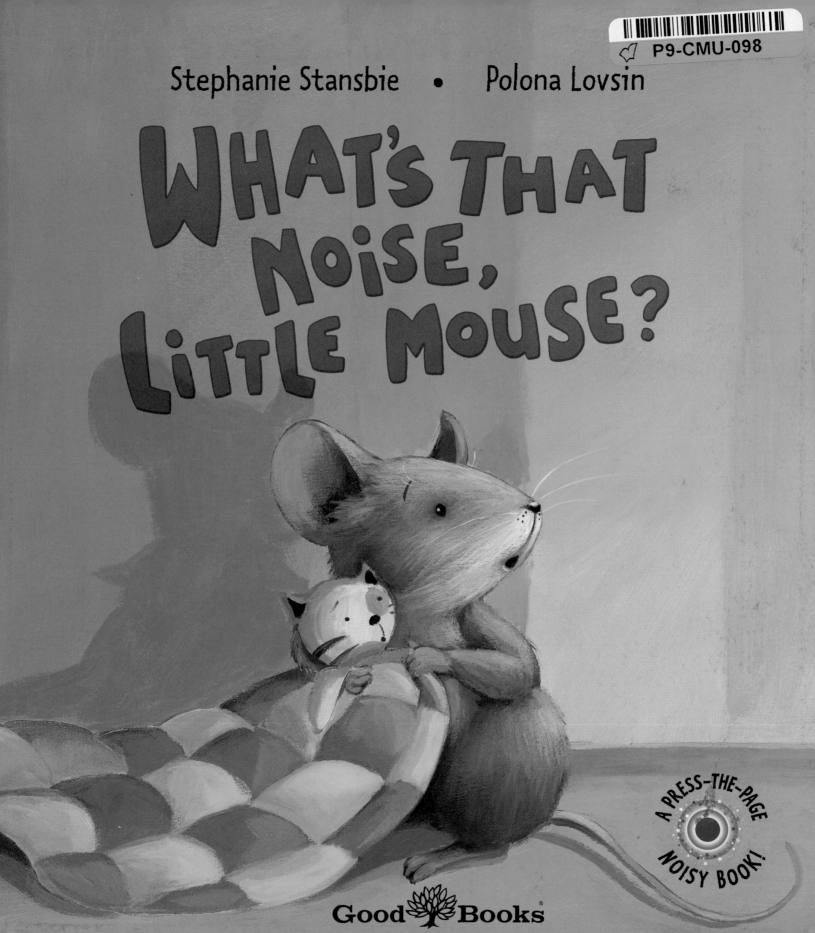

A PRESS-THE-PAGE NOISY BOOK!

Good Books

Intercourse, PA 17534, 800/762-7171, www.GoodBooks.com

The moon was up, the night was still, and Little Mouse
was half asleep. All at once, there came a noise –
a long and loud and trembling sound . . .

"What's that?" cried Mouse, now wide awake, holding his covers tight. But then he heard another noise, a steady tapping in the night . . .

Tick - tock!
Tick - tock!
Tick - tock!

Little Mouse crept out of bed and tiptoed from his room.
His heart was all a-flutter!

Outside, the wind was stirring in the trees,
shaking the leaves with a shivering breeze.
Through the hall window, crisp and clear,
came a bustling,
      rustling,
            whispering sound . . .

Ssssssssssssshhhhhh

"Oh my goodness!" Little Mouse gasped,
and he scrambled downstairs
as fast as he could!

hhhhhhhhhhh!

Standing alone in the kitchen,
Mouse couldn't believe his ears . . .

a wet and wobbly dripping noise dribbled in the dark . . .

Drip!
Drip!
Drip!

"It's a ghost!"
Little Mouse cried,
and he ran and hid
in the cupboard.

The moonlight crept through the cupboard door, casting shadows all around. Little Mouse heard a grating sound – a creaking, squeaking, scraping sound . . .

Crrreeeeeeaaaak!

"The ghost's **coming to get me!**"
Little Mouse wailed.

He raced up the stairs and dived beneath
the covers. But then came the
worst noise of all . . .

a rattling, chattering, clattering
sound – and it was heading straight toward
Little Mouse . . .

Rattle!

Rattle!

Rattle!

Shaking and quaking and quivering and shivering, Little Mouse let out the loudest sound of all . . .

hhhhaaaaaahhhhhhhhh!

Quick as a flash, Mommy Mouse scampered into the room.

"What is it, little one?" she called.

"A g-g-ghost!" Little Mouse cried. "It's louder than loud. Can you hear it?"

"I can hear Owl singing his song,"
said Mommy Mouse.

Too-whoo!
Too-whoo!

"And your little clock ticking
to lull you to sleep."

Tick-tock!
Tick-tock!
Tick-tock!

Ssssshhhhhhhhhhhhhh!

"There's a breeze
in the trees,
wishing you
good night,"

"a kitchen tap dripping,"

Drip!
Drip!
Drip!

"a cupboard door creaking,"

Crreeeeeeeaaaak!

"and your windowpane rattling."

Rattle!
Rattle!
Rattle!

Mommy Mouse smiled . . .

"No ghost, then," said Little Mouse. "I didn't think there was."
Mommy Mouse tucked him in and hugged him close.
"Sweet dreams, sleep tight, wish-my-mouse a quiet night!"
she sang to him softly.

And soon the only noise to be heard
in the whole house . . .

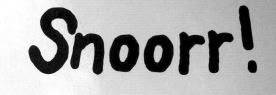

was the **thundering**
sound of a little mouse
snoring!

Snoorr!

Snooorr!

Sssssnnooooorrrr!